The Missing Make-a-Pet!

"Have you guys started playing Petopia yet?" George asked Nancy and Bess. "It's so much fun!"

Nancy nodded. "I know! I can't wait to play again when I get home."

"I'm going to try to win the contest," Bess said. "Itty Bitty needs a new backpack to carry all her kitty treats!"

Just then, Violet came rushing up to Nancy and the girls. She looked upset.

"Violet, what's wrong?" Nancy asked her.

"Everything!" Violet cried out. "Someone stole Hoppity!"

Join the CLUE CREW
& solve these other cases!

#1 *Sleepover Sleuths*

#2 *Scream for Ice Cream*

#3 *Pony Problems*

#4 *The Cinderella Ballet Mystery*

#5 *Case of the Sneaky Snowman*

#6 *The Fashion Disaster*

#7 *The Circus Scare*

#8 *Lights, Camera . . . Cats!*

#9 *The Halloween Hoax*

#10 *Ticket Trouble*

#11 *Ski School Sneak*

#12 *Valentine's Day Secret*

#13 *Chick-napped!*

#14 *The Zoo Crew*

#15 *Mall Madness*

#16 *Thanksgiving Thief*

#17 *Wedding Day Disaster*

#18 *Earth Day Escapade*

#19 *April Fool's Day*

#20 *Treasure Trouble*

#21 *Double Take*

#22 *Unicorn Uproar*

#23 *Babysitting Bandit*

#24 *Princess Mix-up Mystery*

#25 *Buggy Breakout*

#26 *Camp Creepy*

#27 *Cat Burglar Caper*

#28 *Time Thief*

#29 *Designed for Disaster*

#30 *Dance Off*

NANCY DREW
#31 AND THE CLUE CREW®

The Make-a-Pet Mystery

BY CAROLYN KEENE

ILLUSTRATED BY MACKY PAMINTUAN

Aladdin
New York London Toronto Sydney New Delhi

⚲ ALADDIN

An imprint of Simon & Schuster Children's Publishing Division

1230 Avenue of the Americas, New York, NY 10020

First Aladdin paperback edition January 2012

Text copyright © 2012 by Simon & Schuster, Inc.

Illustrations copyright © 2012 by Macky Pamintuan

All rights reserved, including the right of reproduction in whole or in part in any form.

ALADDIN and related logo, NANCY DREW, and NANCY DREW AND THE CLUE CREW are registered trademarks of Simon & Schuster, Inc.

For information about special discounts for bulk purchases, please contact Simon & Schuster Special Sales at 1-866-506-1949 or business@simonandschuster.com.

The Simon & Schuster Speakers Bureau can bring authors to your live event. For more information or to book an event contact the Simon & Schuster Speakers Bureau at 1-866-248-3049 or visit our website at www.simonspeakers.com.

Designed by Lisa Vega

The text of this book was set in ITC Stone Informal.

Manufactured in the United States of America 1211 OFF

10 9 8 7 6 5 4 3 2 1

Library of Congress Control Number 2011939420

ISBN 978-1-4169-9464-0

ISBN 978-1-4424-4620-5 (eBook)

CONTENTS

CHAPTER ONE: MAKE-A-PET · · · · · · · · · · · · · 1

CHAPTER TWO: PETOPIA · · · · · · · · · · · · · · · 8

CHAPTER THREE: A BUNNY THIEF · · · · · · · · · · · 17

CHAPTER FOUR: THE MYSTERIOUS CLUE · · · · · · · 25

CHAPTER FIVE: OUT OF CONTROL · · · · · · · · · · 32

CHAPTER SIX: A NEW SUSPECT · · · · · · · · · · · 41

CHAPTER SEVEN: THE HACKER RETURNS · · · · · · · 48

CHAPTER EIGHT: TWO APOLOGIES · · · · · · · · · · · 59

CHAPTER NINE: ONE MYSTERY SOLVED · · · · · · · 67

CHAPTER TEN: LOST . . . AND FOUND · · · · · · · · 73

CHAPTER ONE

Make-a-Pet

"I can't wait to make my very own puppy," Nancy Drew declared as she headed into the main entrance of the River Heights Mall. She pulled off her hat and mittens and stuffed them into her coat pockets.

"And *I* can't wait to make my very own kitty," Bess Marvin piped up. She did a little twirl as she followed behind Nancy. "She's going to be the most beautiful kitty in the world!"

"Well, *I* can't wait to make my very own tiger," Bess's cousin, George Fayne said. "I already have a name for him: Furrrocious!" She held up her hands on either side of her head, pretending to have big tiger ears.

The three best friends were on their way to a new store at the mall called Make-a-Pet. They had been saving their allowance money for ages so they could each buy—actually, create—their very own Make-a-Pet.

Hannah Gruen had come along with the girls. Hannah worked as a housekeeper for Nancy and her father, although to Nancy she was more like a mother than a housekeeper.

"Hmm, maybe I should make one of these stuffed animals too. They sound like fun," Hannah said, tucking her car keys into her purse.

"It's not a stuffed animal, Hannah. It's a Make-a-Pet!" Nancy corrected her.

Hannah laughed. "Oh! My mistake."

Inside the mall, Nancy paused to figure out where they were going. "Over there!" she said eagerly, pointing to a storefront on the other side of the fountain. The sign said MAKE-A-PET in different-colored letters. Each letter had a different animal on top of it, including a hopping frog, a waddling duck, and a slithering snake. The snake made Nancy shiver a little.

Bess grabbed Nancy's and George's hands and pulled them toward the store.

"No running!" Hannah called after them. "Don't worry, we have plenty of time to make pets before we get pizza!"

Pizza! Normally, Nancy would have been superpsyched about going out for pizza. But right now she was so excited about their Make-a-Pet project that she could hardly think about food—or anything else.

The inside of the Make-a-Pet store was even more fun and colorful than the sign out front. There were shelves full of puppies, kitties, and other animals dressed up in cool outfits. There were lots of tables, too, with kids making their own pets similar to the ones on the shelves. Nancy wasn't sure where to start.

"Are you here to make a pet?" a young woman asked the three girls in a friendly voice. She wore jeans and a red T-shirt with the

Make-a-Pet logo. Her name tag read TABITHA.

"Yes!" Nancy, George, and Bess said at the same time.

"Do you all know what kind of pet you'd like to make?" Tabitha asked them.

Nancy raised her hand. "A puppy!"

"A kitty!" Bess said.

"A bear!" George added.

Tabitha grinned. "Sounds like you girls know what you want. Follow me!"

While Hannah wandered around the store, Tabitha led Nancy, Bess, and George to the first workstation, which had a sign above it that said: STEP 1, PICK YOUR PET! There, they picked out a shell for their pets, which was the outside part with no stuffing inside. Nancy's puppy was cute and brown, like her real puppy back home, Chocolate Chip. But without its stuffing, the puppy looked kind of flat, like a fuzzy sweater.

"Don't worry, we'll get your pets fattened up right away," Tabitha told them. She led them to the second workstation, which had a sign above it that read  STEP 2, FILL UP YOUR PET! Tabitha had to help them with this step, which involved hooking their pets' shells up to a special machine. Within minutes Nancy's puppy was a cuddly stuffed animal that she could squeeze and hug. She couldn't believe it!

At the third workstation—DRESS YOUR PET!—Nancy and her friends ran into some girls they knew: Deirdre Shannon, Madison Foley, and Kendra Jackson, who were in their third-grade class at school.

"Hey, it's the Clueless Crew!" Deirdre exclaimed. "Are you working on a case? What's it called? The Mystery of the Ugly Cat?"

She pointed to Bess's kitty and cracked up.

Bess glared at Deirdre. "Ha-ha, very funny."

Nancy, Bess, and George had a club called the Clue Crew. The Clue Crew solved mysteries—everything from finding missing chicks to tracking down a valuable pet bug. Deirdre, Madison, and Kendra once started a club called the Klue Krew to compete with the Clue Crew, but it didn't last very long.

"Well, my Make-a-Pet is *way* cuter," Deirdre bragged. She held up a lavender mouse. It was wearing a fancy purple dress covered with glittery rhinestones. "Isn't her outfit awesome? It's the most expensive one in the store!"

George rolled her eyes and turned to Madison. "I like your turtle," she said.

"Thanks," Madison said. Her turtle was dressed in an orange baseball jacket and cap.

"And I like your pony, Kendra," Nancy added.

"Thank you," Kendra said. Her pony was dressed in a red satin jacket and matching bow tie.

Nancy, Bess, and George picked out outfits for their pets too. Nancy picked out a light blue sweater for her puppy. Bess picked out a ruffled pink dress for her kitty. And George picked out a black-and-white karate uniform for her bear.

The three girls, along with Deirdre, Madison, and Kendra, moved on to the fourth and final workstation, which was the NAME YOUR PET! station. There they all filled out their pet's names and birth dates for their pets' birth certificates.

Nancy decided to call her puppy Mocha Chip, since it sounded kind of like Chocolate Chip. Bess named her kitty Itty Bitty. George stuck to Furrrocious for her bear.

Deirdre chose Squeak Squeak for her mouse. Madison picked Myrtle the Turtle, and Kendra settled on Prancer for her pony.

Bess filled out Itty Bitty's birth certificate with a sparkly pink pen, dotting the two *i*'s with little hearts. "This is superfun!" she exclaimed.

"This is super*dumb*!" someone muttered.

CHAPTER TWO

Petopia

Nancy glanced up from Mocha Chip's birth certificate with a frown. Who was being so mean and cranky about Make-a-Pets?

It was Catherine Spangler from school. Catherine was walking up to their workstation with a grumpy expression.

"Hi, Catherine!" Nancy said, trying to sound friendly. "Are you here to make a pet too?"

"No way," Catherine said

huffily. "I hate Make-a-Pets. They're for babies."

"Babies?" Deirdre snapped. "I don't think so."

"Well, they are," Catherine insisted.

Nancy noticed that Catherine was carrying a bunch of shopping bags. The bags were from several different stores, including L'il Tots and Babymagic and Toy Mania.

"Wow, you bought a lot of stuff!" Madison remarked, pointing to the bags.

"These aren't mine, they're my mom's. She's making me carry them around the mall because she has to push my baby brother around in his stupid stroller." Catherine stopped and looked out at the mall. "Oh, there she is. I've gotta go. Bye!"

"Bye!" Nancy and the other girls said.

"That was random," Kendra said after Catherine left.

George shrugged. "I guess she really doesn't like Make-a-Pets."

Bess kissed Itty Bitty on the nose. "That doesn't make sense. *Everyone* likes Make-a-Pets!"

Or not, Nancy thought.

"You guys are late!" Deirdre said impatiently. "Come on, come on. Everyone's down in the basement already!"

Nancy walked through the front door, followed by Bess and George. It was Sunday afternoon, and Deirdre had invited them over for a playdate. Nancy had brought Mocha Chip along, and Bess and George had brought Itty Bitty and Furrrocious. Deirdre was holding her Make-a-Pet too. Today, Squeak Squeak was wearing a white dress with red polka dots.

Downstairs, Madison and Kendra were hanging out in the huge, high-tech rec room. Catherine was also there, and so were two other girls from their school, Violet Keeler and Gaby Small. Madison was pretending to feed popcorn to Myrtle the Turtle, and Kendra was galloping Prancer across the sofa. Violet was sitting at a slick white computer punching keys, her Make-a-Pet bunny perched beside her. Gaby was hovering over Violet, her Make-a-Pet chick tucked under her arm. Catherine seemed to be the only one in the room without a Make-a-Pet.

"Hi, Nancy, Bess, and George!" Violet called out. "I'm, uh, lodging on to the computer so we can register our Make-a-Pets!"

"We're *logging* on, dummy," Gaby corrected her. "Have you guys registered your Make-a-Pets yet?" she asked Nancy, Bess, and George.

The three girls glanced at one another, confused. "I didn't know we were supposed to do that," Nancy said.

"Yeah, we're all registering our Make-a-Pets," Deirdre piped up. "They have this cool website."

"Booooring," Catherine complained. She sat down on the sofa and began flipping through a magazine.

"And once we register, we can play this awesome game called Petopia," Gaby said, ignoring Catherine. She nudged Violet. "Here, you're too slow. Let me do that!"

"Whatever," Violet grumbled, scooting over.

Everyone gathered around Gaby as she began typing various commands. Nancy had no idea that Gaby was so good with computers. Within seconds the Make-a-Pet logo appeared, along with a colorful menu with lots of options. Gaby selected the icon that read "Register your pet!"

"Okay, so we can take turns registering our pets," she explained to everyone. "Don't forget, you have to pick a password. Without a password, you won't be able to sign in to your Make-a-Pet account."

The girls did as Gaby instructed, taking turns at the computer to register their Make-a-Pets. When it was Violet's turn, she glanced up at the others. "I can't decide which password I like better for Hoppity— Fluffybunny123 or Carrotcake456," she mused out loud. "What do you guys think?"

"Violet!" Gaby cried out. "Your password is *private*! You can't tell anybody what it is!"

"Oh!" Violet blushed. "Okay. Whatever."

After Violet and all the other girls had finished registering their Make-a-Pets, Gaby sat back down at the computer and showed everyone how to play the Petopia game. The goal of the game was to get as many points as possible by having adventures, finding treasure, and making friends and allies. The players had to overcome obstacles too, like fire-breathing monsters and raging blizzards.

But before they could play, the girls had to create human avatars for themselves. Avatars traveled around the Petopia kingdom with their Make-a-Pets. Nancy picked an avatar who looked like her, with long, reddish-blond hair and blue eyes. She named her avatar Natasha because it sounded like a glamorous spy name.

Once the other girls had picked out their avatars, Gaby demonstrated how each girl could make her avatar and pet travel around Petopia, using the arrows on the keyboard. She added that when the avatars and pets went anywhere in Petopia, they might leave clues to their trail, which could lead other players to track them down. Players could also switch pets, too, with other players in the game.

Nancy was excited. Playing Petopia was going to be fun! She noticed that even cranky Catherine was staring intently at the images flashing across the screen.

"Hey! We should all have a Petopia contest," Gaby suggested.

Deirdre's eyes flashed. "What kind of a contest?"

"Whoever has the highest points at the end of the week wins," Gaby said.

"What's the prize?" Madison asked.

Violet raised her hand. "I know, I know! The losers have to pay a dollar each so the winner can buy a new accessory for her Make-a-Pet. Like one of those cute little scarves."

All the girls nodded eagerly—all except for Catherine, who slumped down on the couch and started flipping through her magazine again.

Deirdre petted Squeak Squeak. "Yay! You're going to get a new scarf!"

"No, *Buttercup*'s going to get a new scarf," Gaby corrected her. She picked up her Make-a-Pet chick and kissed it on its beak. "I'm the best one at computers, so I'm definitely going to win."

"Win what?"

Nancy turned around and saw Sonia Susi bounding down the stairs. Sonia, too, was in their class at River Heights Elementary School.

"Win our Petopia contest," Kendra explained. She told Sonia all about the Petopia game and the contest rules they had just agreed on.

"That sounds cool," Sonia said when Kendra had finished.

"Yeah. If I win, I'm going to buy Hoppity this

scarf I saw. It has a carrot design on it," Violet said eagerly.

Sonia gasped. "Violet! You're a thief!" she burst out.

ChaPTER ThRE

A Bunny Thief

Violet turned pale. "A thief? Sonia, what are you talking about?"

Sonia pointed to Hoppity. "*That.* You stole my Make-a-Pet!"

"That's *your* bunny?" Nancy asked Sonia, surprised.

"Yes! I mean, no! I mean, s-sort of!" Sonia stammered.

Nancy frowned. This was getting confusing. "How can Hoppity 'sort of' be your bunny?"

"Well, I don't have a Make-a-Pet . . . yet," Sonia explained. "I still need four more dollars, which I'm getting tonight, since it's allowance night. My mom's taking me to the mall after dinner to get my bunny." She narrowed her eyes at Violet. "Violet knew that. *And* she knew that I was going to name my bunny Hoppity."

"Who cares? Sonia, just pick a different name." Deirdre fluffed Squeak Squeak's dress.

"But it's *my* name!" Sonia insisted.

"No, it's *mine*!" Violet cried out. She clutched the bunny to her chest.

"*I* thought of it first!"

"No, *I* did!"

The two girls continued arguing. Nancy glanced at Sonia and then at Violet, wondering who was telling the truth . . . and who was not.

Monday was show-and-tell day at school. Michael Dorf was standing up front, making his presentation.

"My super-duper bubble machine can make bubbles in all different sizes—and colors, too," he said. "I can also make bubbles with different fragrances. That means 'smells.' So far I've made bubbles that smell like peppermint, chocolate, and broccoli. And that concludes my show-and-tell presentation."

"Broccoli?" George turned around and whispered to Nancy. Nancy shrugged.

Mrs. Ramirez smiled. "Thanks, Michael D. I think that's one of your most interesting inventions yet. Who wants to go next?"

Luna Valeri raised her hand. "I do! Can I show everyone my new Make-a-Pet ladybug?"

"But what about my amazing new Make-a-Pet camel?" Michael Lawrence piped up. Everyone called him "Michael L.," to tell him apart from Michael D.

"I think *I* should go next," Nadine Nardo said. "My Make-a-Pet poodle can do tricks!"

A dozen other kids raised their hands. Nancy noticed that they all had Make-a-Pets.

Antonio Elefano, who sat across from Nancy, rolled his eyes. "What's up with these Make-a-Pets? They're laaaaame."

Bess, who sat in front of Antonio, whirled around. "You're just jealous because you don't have one!" she said in a low, angry voice.

"Yeah? I have something better. I have Killerosaurus!" Antonio pulled a large green plastic dinosaur out of his backpack. "And Killerosaurus is gonna eat your Fake-a-Pet for lunch! *Grrrrrr!*"

"Oh, no, he isn't!" Bess hid Itty Bitty in her lap.

"Antonio, please put your dinosaur away," Mrs. Ramirez told him sternly. "And let's see . . . Sonia! Why don't you go next?"

"Uh, okay. I guess," Sonia said reluctantly. "This is my squirrel." She stood up and held out a stuffed squirrel. It was wearing a T-shirt that read I'M NUTS FOR NUTS. "His name is Squirrel." She started to sit back down.

"Hang on, Sonia. Tell us a little something about Squirrel," Mrs. Ramirez urged. "Where did you get him? Are squirrels your favorite kind of animal?"

"I got him at the mall last night at the Make-a-Pet store. And no, squirrels *aren't* my favorite. Bunnies are." Sonia stared pointedly at Violet.

Violet glared back at Sonia. She hugged Hoppity to her chest.

"Oh! But squirrels are wonderful animals too," Mrs. Ramirez said, looking confused. "They're very cute. They have very good vision, and they can grasp things really well with their claws."

"If you say so." Sonia tugged at her short blonde hair.

"Okay, well . . . thank you, Sonia. Who wants to go next? Catherine?" Mrs. Ramirez suggested.

Catherine went up to the front of the class with a tiny blue bear that was too small to be a Make-a-Pet. As she began her presentation, Nancy glanced over at Sonia. Sonia had carelessly tossed Squirrel into her backpack and was doodling in her notebook with a glum expression.

Nancy wondered, *What is it going to take to make Sonia feel better about not having a Make-a-Pet bunny named Hoppity?*

"I'm ready for ice cream!" Bess announced. She waltzed up to Nancy's cubby.

"Me too!" George said, following behind. The two cousins were wearing their coats, hats, and mittens and carrying their backpacks.

"Me three!" Nancy said, slipping on her parka. The last bell had just rung, and the hallway was jammed with kids. Hannah was meeting Nancy, Bess, and George in a few minutes to take them to Double Dip, their favorite ice-cream parlor.

"That's dumb. Who wants to eat ice cream in January?" Michael L. called out from his cubby.

Bess giggled. "Any month is good for ice cream!"

"Have you guys started playing Petopia yet?" George asked Nancy and Bess. "It's so much fun!"

Nancy nodded. "I know! I can't wait to play again when I get home."

"I'm going to try to win the contest," Bess said. "Itty Bitty needs a new backpack to carry all her kitty treats!"

Just then, Violet came rushing up to Nancy and the girls. She looked upset.

"Violet, what's wrong?" Nancy asked her.

"Everything!" Violet cried out. "Someone stole Hoppity!"

CHAPTER FOUR

The Mysterious Clue

"What do you mean, someone stole Hoppity?" Nancy demanded.

"Just what I said. I left Hoppity in my cubby. And now she's gone!" Violet's eyes shimmered with tears.

"Are you sure you didn't put her somewhere else, and you just forgot?" Bess piped up.

Violet shook her head. "No, I definitely put her in my cubby."

Nancy thought this over. "When was the last time you saw her?" she said finally.

"Hmm . . . I put her in my cubby right after show-and-tell," Violet replied. "Then at lunchtime I went to give her a pretend carrot. That was the last time, I think."

"Lunchtime. That means that someone had, like, three hours to sneak Hoppity out of your cubby," Nancy said.

Violet nodded in agreement. Then her face lit up. "Hey, I just remembered! You guys are secret agents!"

Nancy grinned. "You mean detectives?"

"Yes, that! So I can hire you to get Hoppity back for me, right? Puh-leeeeease?" Violet begged. "I'll pay you whatever you want! I have twelve dollars and twenty-eight . . . no, twenty-*nine* cents in my piggy bank."

"We don't charge," George told her. "And we'll take your case! If it's okay with you guys," she said quickly to Nancy and Bess.

"I'm in," Nancy said.

"I'm in too," Bess added.

"Yay! Thank you! So what do we do now?" Violet said eagerly.

"First we should check the scene of the crime for clues," Nancy said.

"The . . . scene of the what?" Violet asked.

"The scene of the crime. That means your cubby," Bess explained.

"Oh!" Violet nodded. "Okay. Follow me!"

The four girls walked over to Violet's cubby. Nancy knew that Hannah was probably waiting outside for her, Bess, and George to take them to Double Dip. So they had to work fast.

Nancy started searching through Violet's cubby. The hallway was practically empty; almost everyone had left for home by now.

On the walls of Violet's cubby were magazine clippings of pop star Lula Rappaport, who Nancy knew was Violet's favorite singer. Hanging on the hook were Violet's backpack, which had Lula stickers all over it, and Violet's hot-pink jacket.

Nancy knelt down to search the bottom of the cubby. There were pencils, pens, a couple of notebooks, and a Lula fan magazine. Then she noticed something else, way in the back. She picked it up.

It was a small, doughnut-shaped object. It was clear blue, and it felt soft and squishy. What could it be?

"Is this yours?" Nancy asked Violet.

"Um, no. I don't even know what it is," Violet replied.

"It looks like a doll bracelet or something," Bess remarked.

"I think I've seen one of those before," George said slowly. "Or maybe not. I'm not sure. I'll try to remember."

"Thanks, George." Nancy reached into her backpack, pulled out a plastic bag, and dropped the blue doughnut into it. She kept a bunch of such bags in her backpack, for storing clues. "Our first clue!" she announced.

"Except that our clue is a mystery too, since we don't know what it is," Bess joked.

"So let's talk about motives," Nancy said as she dug into her Crazilicious Caramel sundae.

Nancy, Bess, George, and Violet were sitting in a booth at Double Dip. Violet had gotten permission from her parents to come along too. Hannah was at a table across from the four girls, talking to an old friend she had run into.

"Motives?" Violet repeated. "What are

motives?" She licked chocolate syrup off of her spoon.

"A motive is why someone does something," Bess explained. She plucked a cherry from the top of her Bananarama sundae. "Like, why would someone want to steal Hoppity?"

"Because she's the most awesome bunny in the entire world?" Violet said. "Obviously?"

George took a sip of her Very, Very Berry shake. "That's a good motive. What about suspects?"

"I think Antonio did it. He's evil!" Bess exclaimed. "His Killer-whatever almost ate Itty Bitty!"

Nancy had been wondering about Antonio too. He was famous for pulling mean pranks on his classmates.

"We should definitely add Antonio to the suspect list," Nancy agreed. "What about Sonia?"

"Sonia?" Violet shook her head. "No way!"

"But aren't you two fighting?" George said.

Violet put her spoon down with a clatter. She looked upset. "No! Sonia and I are, like, best friends. She would never steal Hoppity!" She added, "Besides, best friends have fights once in a while. It's no big deal."

"But she said you stole her idea about getting a Make-a-Pet bunny and naming her Hoppity," George persisted.

"Is Sonia right? *Did* you steal her idea about Hoppity?" Nancy asked Violet gently.

"No!" Violet insisted. But she wouldn't meet Nancy's gaze.

Hmm, Nancy thought. *Violet's keeping something from us. What is it?*

CHAPTER FIVE

Out of Control

"There's Sonia," Nancy said, pointing to the swings. "Let's go talk to her!"

It was Tuesday at recess. Even though it was January, the weather was nice, so the students had bundled up and headed outside after lunch. As Nancy, Bess, and George half walked, half ran across the playground, their boots kicked up clouds of fluffy snow. They passed groups of kids playing hopscotch, kickball, and other games.

"So what are we going to say to her?" George asked Nancy.

"Well, we shouldn't let her know that she's a suspect," Nancy replied.

The three girls slowed their steps as they neared the swing set. Sonia was pumping her legs hard to make herself go way up high.

"Hey, Sonia!" Nancy said, waving.

Sonia waved back. "Hey! Do you want a turn?" she called out, dragging her heels along the ground.

"No. We just wanted to talk to you," Nancy said.

Sonia frowned. "Uh . . . what about?"

Bess put her hands on her hips. "We know you stole Hoppity from Violet's cubby, Sonia Susi! Where is she? Where are you hiding her? And how could you do that to your best friend?" she demanded.

"Bess!" Nancy whispered.

"What? Hoppity's missing?" Sonia exclaimed.

"Don't act surprised! You know perfectly well that—" Bess began.

"*Bess!*" Nancy poked her friend with her elbow. "Someone stole Hoppity from Violet's cubby yesterday," she explained to Sonia. "We thought maybe you might know something. Or maybe you saw something?"

"No," Sonia replied. "Omigosh, this is awful! Violet must be so upset."

Nancy pulled the blue doughnut out of her pocket. "Is this yours?" she asked Sonia.

Sonia squinted at the doughnut, then shook her head. "No. What is it? It's weird-looking."

"We're not sure what it is," George admitted.

"Where were you between lunch and the end of school yesterday, Sonia?" Bess demanded.

"I was in class! With *you* guys!" Sonia pointed out. "Why are you asking me all these questions? Do you really think I would steal Hoppity?"

"Well, you told everyone at Deirdre's house that *Violet* kind of stole Hoppity from *you*," Bess said. "Maybe you were getting back at her for that."

"I would never!" Sonia cried out. She jumped off the swing and started heading toward the door. "I'm not going to talk to you guys anymore. You're mean!" she complained.

Nancy watched Sonia as she stormed off. Was Sonia telling the truth? Or was she hiding something—just like Violet?

"I think Sonia should be our number one suspect," Bess declared.

It was after school on Tuesday. She, Nancy, and

George were in Nancy's bedroom going over the case. Hannah had made them a big bowl of buttery popcorn and mugs of hot apple cider. She always gave them extra-yummy snacks when they were hard at work on a new mystery.

"I think so too," George agreed. She was sitting at Nancy's desk. Furrrocious was propped up next to the computer, looking ferocious in his karate uniform. "Nancy, what do you think?"

"I think we should start writing down all this stuff," Nancy replied. She reached into her backpack and pulled out her purple notebook. She used it to keep track of the Clue Crew's cases. "George, do you want to start a new file, too?"

"I'm on it." George turned to the keyboard and began typing. She liked to record the Clue Crew's clues and suspects on the computer. "After we're done with this, maybe we could play Petopia?" she said hopefully.

"Yes!" Bess said, hugging Itty Bitty to her chest. "I didn't get to play yesterday because I had other stuff I had to do."

"Yeah, me too. We need to catch up!" Nancy agreed.

Nancy flipped to a clean page in her notebook. Where should she begin? She glanced around her lavender-and-white room as she thought about what to write. She grinned at Mocha Chip, who was lying in a doll-size bed next to Chocolate Chip, who was lying in a puppy-size bed. It was fun having a Make-a-Pet *and* a real pet!

Then she picked up her purple pen and wrote:

SUSPECTS

-Sonia Susi. She said that SHE came up with the idea about a Make-a-Pet bunny named Hoppity. She said that Violet stole the idea from her. Maybe she feels that Hoppity really belongs to her?

-Antonio Elefano. He likes practical jokes. Maybe stealing Hoppity was a practical joke?

"Can you think of any other suspects besides Sonia and Antonio?" Nancy asked Bess and George.

Bess shook her head. "Nope. We have a clue, though. The squishy blue thingy!"

"Yes!" Nancy turned to the next page and wrote:

CLUES

-The blue "doughnut." We found it at the
bottom of Violet's cubby the same day
Hoppity disappeared. Maybe Hoppity's thief
dropped it by accident?

"George, you said that maybe you saw it
before, somewhere?" Nancy asked her.

"Yup. I still think I did. I just can't remember
for sure," George replied.

Bess sat up, her blue eyes flashing. "Hey! You
know how I said yesterday that it looked like
a dolly bracelet? So maybe it's a bracelet for a
Make-a-Pet! When we were at the Make-a-Pet
store on Saturday, they had a bunch of jewelry
for the pets."

"Bess, you're a genius!" Nancy told her.

"I'll check the Make-a-Pet website and see
if they have it at their online store," George
offered.

Just then, Nancy heard a familiar *ting!* sound

on her computer. An instant message window popped up on the screen.

"It's from Violet," George announced. She scanned the message quickly. "Uh-oh."

"What?" Nancy jumped to her feet and began reading the message over George's shoulder. Bess did the same.

Violet had written:

HELP!!!!!!! Something weird is happening with my Petopia game. My avatar is totally out of control!!!!!!!

ChaPTER Six

A New Suspect

"What does Violet mean, her avatar is totally out of control?" Bess said, confused.

"George, can you ask Violet?" Nancy said.

"Sure." George typed:

Hi. It's George. Bess and Nancy are with me. What's going on?

Violet wrote back:

Princess Pompom (that's my avatar's name) and Hoppity (the computer Hoppity, not the real Hoppity) are doing all kinds of stupid stuff. Like picking fights with friends. And making dumb mistakes on purpose. And not collecting treasure when they're supposed to. They're losing points like crazy!!!!!!!

"Maybe Violet's not very good at the Petopia game," Bess said, shrugging.

"Maybe," George said. She typed:

We don't understand. Are you making Princess Pompom and computer Hoppity do this stuff?

Violet wrote back:

NO!!!!!!! That's what's crazy. It's like someone is lodging in as me and playing the game when I'm not playing and making Princess Pompom and computer Hoppity do this stuff.

Nancy, Bess, and George exchanged glances. "Are you guys thinking what I'm thinking?" Nancy said after a moment.

George nodded. "Someone got Violet's secret password!"

Bess rolled her eyes. "Well, that wouldn't be hard! She was practically telling everyone what it was, over at Deirdre's house. Remember? And then she *kept* talking about it the whole time we were there, even after Gaby told her to stop."

"Oh yeah." Nancy recalled Violet asking the other girls which password was better,

Fluffy-something or Carrot-something. "George, can you ask Violet if she picked one of those passwords she was talking about at Deirdre's?"

George nodded and typed the message. A moment later Violet wrote back:

Yes, I picked Carrotcake456. I thought it would be easier to remember than Fluffybunny123 because carrot cake is my favorite dessert! And my birthday is April, which is 4! And 5 and 6 come after 4!

Violet added:

Why—was that dumb? Should I change my password or something?

"Uh, yeah," Bess said, rolling her eyes again.

Nancy held up her hand. "No! George, tell Violet not to change it."

"Why not?" George asked Nancy. "If she doesn't change it, the person is just going to keep lodging—I mean, *logging* in to Violet's account and messing up her Petopia game. Right?"

"That's exactly what we want," Nancy replied. "Maybe the person will make a mistake and leave a clue. And we might be able to

43

figure out who she is. Or he," she added quickly, thinking of Antonio. Except, Antonio wasn't at Deirdre's house on Sunday. So how would he know Violet's password?

"Nancy, you're brilliant!" George said. She began typing another message to Violet.

"Watch out, Natasha!" Nancy cried out.

Nancy repeatedly tapped the up arrow on her keyboard to make her Petopia avatar run and jump. On the screen, Natasha and the cyber Mocha Chip, which was another name for the computer Mocha Chip, leaped off the cobblestone path and into a fizzleberry bush—just in time to avoid a fire-breathing dragon.

It was after dinner, and Nancy was in her cozy blue pajamas. Her father had given her permission to play a few minutes of Petopia before going to bed.

The only other time she had played Petopia was on Sunday night, after coming home from Deirdre's. Since then, Nancy's avatar, Natasha, and the cyber Mocha Chip had made three friends, completed one quest, and uncovered four pieces of treasure. As a result, Nancy had collected a total of twenty-four points. She wasn't sure how many more points she would need by the end of the week to win the contest—and a new backpack for Mocha Chip. But it was probably a lot more than twenty-four. She knew from IM'ing with George and Bess a few minutes ago that George had thirty-five points and Bess had twenty-three.

But at the moment, Nancy wasn't thinking about winning the contest. She was thinking about the Clue Crew's case.

George had said in her IM that she'd heard Gaby already had forty-nine points—the highest of any of the girls. *Gaby really, really, really wants to win the contest,* George had written.

Nancy sat back in her chair and stared at her computer screen, looking at the image of Natasha and the cyber Mocha Chip hiding in the fizzleberry bush. She thought about Gaby and her amazing computer skills.

Could Gaby have broken into Violet's account and messed up her game? Nancy wondered. *But why? Or maybe Gaby isn't just after Violet. Maybe Gaby is planning on messing up everyone's games so she can win the contest.*

Then something else occurred to Nancy.

Could Gaby have stolen Hoppity too? And is she planning on stealing everyone else's Make-a-Pets?

ChaPTER SEVEN

The Hacker Returns

"But Gaby already has a Make-a-Pet," Bess said at lunchtime the next day. "Her chick, Butterball."

"I think it's Butter*cup*," Nancy corrected her. "But you're right. So why would she want to steal Hoppity?"

George bit into her peanut butter and jelly sandwich. "Maybe she doesn't really want Hoppity," she said after a moment. "Maybe she's just trying to cause trouble so she can win the contest."

"Huh? How can she win the contest by causing trouble?" Bess asked her.

"Because we'd all be too busy looking for

missing Make-a-Pets and trying to figure out who's messing up people's Petopia games," George explained. "And while we're doing that, she'd be scoring major Petopia points."

"That's a really good theory," Nancy said. "I know! Why don't we talk to some of the other girls and see if they've had any problems with their Petopia games? Like if someone's been logging in to their accounts and making their avatars and pets do weird stuff?"

"Good idea," George agreed.

Nancy pulled the blue doughnut out of her backpack. "Plus, I want to see if this belongs to anybody."

"*Whatever* it is," Bess said with a shrug.

Nancy glanced around the cafeteria. She remembered that Sonia was out sick today. She spotted Deirdre, Kendra, and Madison sitting across the aisle. They had their Make-a-Pets with them: Deirdre had her mouse, Kendra had her pony, and Madison had her turtle.

Nancy walked up to them, followed by Bess

and George. "Hey, guys!" she called out.

"Hey, Clueless Crew!" Deirdre said cheerfully. "We're kind of busy right now. Kendra and Madison are helping me figure out which backpack to buy for Squeak Squeak when I win the Petopia contest!"

Kendra and Madison exchanged a funny look.

"That's great, Deirdre. How many points do you have so far?" Nancy asked her.

"Uh, well, a *lot*," Deirdre said, flipping her ponytail over her shoulders. "I'm sure it's *way* more than you have."

Bess put her hands on her hips and started to say something to Deirdre. Nancy elbowed her. "So we were wondering . . . does this belong to any of you guys?" she said, holding out the blue doughnut.

Deirdre made a face. "Uh, no? What *is* that, anyway?"

"It looks like a dog toy," Kendra spoke up.

"Or food from outer space," Madison added. The three girls cracked up.

Okay, so much for that, Nancy thought. "We were wondering about something else too. Have you guys noticed anything funny with your Petopia games?"

"What do you mean, 'anything funny'?" Kendra said.

"You know, like, your avatar doing stuff you didn't tell it to do," George explained.

Deirdre, Kendra, and Madison all shook their heads. "Why, is *your* avatar doing stuff like that?" Deirdre asked George. "That's probably because you don't know how to play the game right!"

"Okay, well, thanks anyway!" Nancy said quickly, dragging George and Bess away. She didn't want to waste time arguing with Deirdre about who was better at Petopia.

"Why is Deirdre so rude sometimes and so nice sometimes?" Bess whispered as they walked away. "She's confusing!"

"She's Deirdre," George said simply.

Just then, the three girls passed Catherine, who was sitting at table by herself and doodling in a notebook.

Pausing, Nancy saw that she was drawing pictures of bunnies dressed in different colorful outfits: a pink ballet tutu, purple pajamas, and a flowery party dress.

"Your bunnies are supercute," Nancy said. "Are they Make-a-Pets?"

Catherine's cheeks flushed red. She slammed her notebook shut. "No!" she said, sounding annoyed. "I'm designing a new line, called . . . uh . . . Create-a-Pets. Yeah, that's right, Create-a-Pets! They're going to be way better than Make-a-Pets. Their clothes are going to be way better too."

"Oh! That sounds cool," Bess said eagerly. "Can I see your designs? I love fashion, so I could maybe help you with—"

"No thanks," Catherine said shortly. She turned away and opened her notebook at a weird angle so that her drawings were hidden from the girls' view.

"Ooookay," George whispered as they walked away. "What's up with Catherine today?"

"Or lately," Bess added. "She's been super-cranky!"

"Hey, guys! Guess how many Petopia points I have so far? *Seventy-five!*"

Nancy turned around. Gaby was standing there. She was clutching a book against her chest called *How to Win at Petopia*.

"Hi, Gaby," Nancy said, waving. Bess and George waved too.

Hi! So I'm totally going to get first place," Gaby said smugly.

"You're totally going to get first place because you're cheating!" Bess blurted out.

"*Bess!*" Nancy and George said at the same time.

"Cheating? Bess, what are you talking about?" Gaby looked shocked.

"You're hacking into people's Petopia accounts," Bess fumed. "Well, Violet's, anyway. So *far.* And you stole Hoppity! Are you going to try to steal Itty Bitty, too? And everyone else's Make-a-Pets? You have a lot of nerve, Gaby Small!"

"*What?*" Gaby gasped. "That makes, like, zero sense! I've had the most Petopia points of anybody since day one. I don't need to hack or steal or whatever to win. I'm the best one at computers in our whole class. Maybe in our whole school!"

Nancy looked at Gaby, wondering if she was telling the truth. Or if maybe she was as good at lying as she was at computers.

"Carrotcake456," Violet said, typing her password into George's computer. "Isn't that the best password ever? I didn't change it, just like you guys said. But if I ever have to, I think I might change it to something totally different. I was thinking maybe Chocolatemilkshake789."

It was after school, and Nancy, Bess, George, and Violet had all gone over to George's house to work on the case. Nancy and her friends had updated Violet on the day's events, including their lunchtime conversations with Deirdre, Kendra, Madison, and Gaby.

"So you think Gaby might be the hacker?" Violet said.

"Maybe. Maybe not." Nancy stared at the screen as the words "Welcome, Princess Pompom and Hoppity!" flashed across a bright green background. "When was the last time you played Petopia?"

"Not since I IM'd with you guys yesterday," Violet replied.

"Okay. Why don't you open up your game and start playing? We can see if the hacker's been back," Nancy suggested.

"Sure!" Violet typed several commands. After a moment, a gloomy landscape spilled across the screen. Dark storm clouds hung over a churning gray river.

"The hacker's definitely been back!" Violet said. She pointed to two figures sitting on the riverbank. "Princess Pompom, what have you *done*? Omigosh, I think she dumped all her treasure into the river. Not that she had a lot to begin with. And Hoppity ate too many carrots, and now she's too fat to move!" she added.

Nancy leaned forward and studied the screen carefully. Violet was right. Her Petopia game was not going well. Her avatar—a tiny, red-haired princess—was sitting next to an empty treasure chest. And the cyber Hoppity was lying belly-up next to an enormous pile of frilly green carrot tops.

"You didn't make Princess Pompom and Hoppity do that?" Bess asked Violet.

"No way!" Violet said. "Ugh. Things were bad enough yesterday when I signed on. And now they're getting worse. . . ."

As Violet talked, Nancy noticed something next to the enormous pile of frilly green carrot tops. She stared at it closely.

It was a squirrel. But Violet's avatar was still on the screen.

"I think I know who our hacker is," Nancy said suddenly.

CHAPTER EIGHT

Two Apologies

"Who is it, Nancy?" Violet demanded. "Who's the hacker?"

"Check it out," Nancy said, pointing to the screen. "You don't have another pet in Petopia, right?"

Violet shook her head. "No. But who else is playing under my name?"

"Someone with a Make-a-Pet squirrel," Nancy replied mysteriously. "Remember? Gaby told us that your avatar and pet can leave clues in the Petopia world."

"*Sonia!*" Bess and George said at the same time.

Violet gasped. "Sonia stole Hoppity! *And* she's the hacker!"

"Me play game too!"

Nancy turned around. George's little brother, Scott, was standing in the doorway. He was dressed in a jelly-stained T-shirt and a diaper with cartoon characters on it.

"Me play pretty game!" Scott shouted, pointing to the computer screen. *"Mine!"*

"Scott, no! We're busy. Mom, Scotty's bothering us!" George called out. She reached

into her desk drawer and pulled out a small plastic dinosaur. "Here, you put this in my coat pocket. Go find Mommy. Okay?"

"'K." Scott grabbed the dinosaur from George and toddled off. Nancy heard George's mother in the hallway speaking to him.

"He's always hiding his toys and stuff in my pockets," George explained, closing the desk drawer. "Sorry about that! Anyway, so . . . what do we do now?"

"I think we should go talk to Sonia," Nancy replied. "We need to get some answers. Like, right away."

Nancy, Bess, George, and Violet all received permission from their parents to walk over to Sonia's house. Sonia lived two blocks away from George.

When the four girls reached the Susi family's sprawling Victorian house, Nancy rang the doorbell. After a moment the door opened.

Sonia was standing there, wearing pink pajamas and a gray hoodie.

"W-what are you guys doing here?" Sonia said, looking startled. Her gaze fell on Violet. "Oh, hey, Violet."

Violet folded her arms across her chest and glared at Sonia. She didn't say anything.

"You were out sick today. Are you okay?" Nancy asked Sonia.

"I had a really bad tummyache from eating too much pizza last night. I'm better now, though," Sonia replied. "Do you guys want to come in?"

"Sure," George said. "We have to talk to you. It's superimportant."

"Uh . . . okay." Sonia led Nancy and her friends into the living room. "Do you guys want a soda or some juice or—Bess, what are you *doing*?"

Bess had gotten down on her hands and knees and was peering under the couch. "I'm looking for Hoppity," she mumbled. "Where are you hiding her, Sonia? Come on, we know you're the thief! Confess!"

Sonia gasped. "I'm not—I didn't—Bess, what are you talking about?"

"The acorns," Nancy said simply. "We know you hacked into Violet's Petopia game."

Sonia turned pale. "Acorns? What acorns? What are you talking about?"

"Didn't you know? When you hacked into Violet's Petopia game, you accidentally left acorn clues behind," George explained.

Sonia glanced away, then sank down onto the couch. "Oops."

"So you admit you're guilty?" Violet demanded.

Sonia nodded slowly.

"Aha!" Violet cried out.

"I'm really, really, *really* sorry," Sonia apologized. "It's just that . . . well, I was so mad at you for stealing my idea about Hoppity."

Now it was Violet's turn to glance away.

"I told you last week how much I wanted a

Make-a-Pet bunny named Hoppity," Sonia went on. "How could you steal my idea, Violet?"

Violet's lip quivered. "The thing is . . . I was at the Make-a-Pet store, and I saw the bunnies on the shelf," she said finally. "They were soooo cute, I felt like I just had to get one! I *had* to! And then I couldn't think of a name for her. But I remembered you mentioning Hoppity, and it was like the perfect, perfect, *perfect* name for my bunny. I didn't think you'd mind if I just kind of borrowed it. . . ."

"You should have asked me first," Sonia pointed out.

"I know, I know. I'm really, really, *really* sorry," Violet apologized. "So . . . is that why you hacked into my Petopia game?"

"Uh-huh. I thought it was the perfect revenge plan," Sonia admitted. "So where *is* Hoppity?" Nancy asked Sonia.

"I didn't steal Hoppity!" Sonia said quickly. "I messed up Violet's Petopia game. That's all."

Nancy, Bess, and George looked at each other. "So if you didn't steal Hoppity, Sonia, then who did?" Bess said finally.

"I don't know," Sonia said. "But tell me what I can do to help you guys find her. I'll do anything!"

Nancy thought for a moment. Then she pulled the blue doughnut out of her backpack. "This is our only clue so far. We found it in Violet's cubby on Monday, when Hoppity disappeared. We can't figure out what it is, though. Do you have any ideas?"

Sonia took the blue doughnut from Nancy. Her eyes lit up. "I know exactly what this is!" she announced.

CHAPTER NINE

One Mystery Solved

"You do?" Nancy said eagerly.

"What is it?" Bess asked Sonia. "Is it a doll bracelet or a doggy toy or food from outer space or . . ."

Sonia shook her head. "None of the above. It's a teething ring."

"A . . . what?" Violet said.

"A teething ring," Sonia repeated. "My little sister, Eden, used to have one when she was a baby."

George nodded excitedly. "Yes! *That's* where I recognize it from! My little brother, Scott, used to have one too! Except his was a *green* doughnut."

"What are they for?" Nancy asked Sonia and George.

"When babies get teeth for the first time, their gums hurt a lot, I guess," George replied. "So my parents would freeze these things, and Scotty would chew on them, and it would make his gums feel better."

"Yeah, same with Eden," Sonia added.

Bess began jumping up and down. "Yay! Mystery solved!" she crowed.

"Wait a second. Back up. So why would the thief leave a teething ring in my cubby?" Violet said, looking confused.

"Maybe your thief is a baby," George joked.

"Funny. Seriously, though. Who left the teething ring in Violet's cubby, and why?" Nancy asked Bess and George.

"Well . . . the thief probably dropped it there by accident, right?" George mused. "The question is, why was the thief carrying a teething ring around?"

❅ ❅ ❅

"So how is your big case going?" Carson Drew asked Nancy. "Have you figured out who did it yet?"

"Not yet, Daddy!" Nancy said.

Nancy picked up her taco and took a big bite. It was make-your-own-taco night at the Drew house. Hannah had laid out plates of yummy shredded cheese, beans, salsa, yellow rice, sliced avocados, and corn tortillas in a line.

On the table next to her plate was Mocha Chip. Tonight Nancy had dressed him in his

light-blue sweater that she had bought at the Make-a-Pet store.

"As of a few nights ago, you had a couple of suspects, right, honey?" Hannah said. "Sonia from your class? And that Antonio boy? The one who put a fake spider in my purse once?"

"Yup," Nancy replied. She went on to explain how the case had gotten more complicated because of the hacker. She added that Sonia had admitted to being the hacker, but not to stealing Hoppity. Which meant that the bunny thief was still on the loose.

"It *could* be Antonio," Nancy finished. "We put Gaby Small on the suspect list too because she really wants to win the Petopia contest! She might have stolen Hoppity to confuse everybody and score lots of points."

"Well, it sounds like the Clue Crew has made a lot of progress," Carson said. "Do you girls have any clues?"

Nancy nodded eagerly. "We found this blue plastic doughnut in Violet's cubby. We figured the thief dropped it there by accident. But we didn't know what it was . . . until today. See, Sonia has a little sister, and she explained that the doughnut was something babies use, called a teething ring."

"Oh, yes . . . teething rings! You used to have one of those," Carson said. "Let's see . . . it was yellow and shaped like an apple."

Nancy grinned. "Really?"

"Really. One day we couldn't find it, and you were so upset that your mom had to go to the drug store and buy you another one right away," Carson said.

Nancy smiled. She liked hearing stories about her mother.

Hanna took a sip of her iced tea. "I bet your thief has a little baby sister or brother," she said to Nancy. "And for whatever reason, your thief happened to be carrying the teething ring around. Maybe it was in the thief's pocket?"

"Hannah, you should be a detective!" Carson complimented her.

Nancy thought about Hannah's idea. *Does Antonio have a baby sister or brother? Or does Gaby?* She didn't think either one of them did, but she wasn't one hundred percent sure.

And then she remembered something— something important. When she, Bess, and George were at the mall on Saturday getting their Make-a-Pets, *someone* was carrying shopping bags from baby stores and complaining a lot.

"I think I know who the thief might be," Nancy said, jumping up from her chair. "I need to call Bess and George right away!"

CHAPTER TEN

Lost . . . and Found

"So you really think Catherine might be the thief?" George said the next afternoon.

"That would totally explain why she's been acting so weird lately," Bess added.

Nancy, Bess, and George were standing in the hallway after school, waiting for Catherine to show up at her cubby. They had tried to talk to her earlier in the day, but she had somehow managed to avoid them, mumbling vaguely that she was "too busy."

"I'm not one hundred percent sure it's her," Nancy said in a low voice. She stepped aside to let a group of kids pass by. "But I *am* sure she has a baby brother. She said so. And she was in such a bad mood at the mall and at Deirdre's house! She's been acting like she doesn't like Make-a-Pets. But maybe she *does* like them and she decided to steal Hoppity?"

"She was drawing those cute little bunnies in her notebook," Bess piped up. "She told us she was designing a new line. But maybe she was lying. Maybe she was designing outfits for Hoppity!"

"If she wanted a Make-a-Pet bunny, why didn't she just buy one?" George pointed out.

Nancy shrugged. "I'm not sure. That's what we have to find out. Oh, hey, there she is!"

Catherine was walking down the hall toward the cubbies, her head buried in a notebook. Nancy saw that it was the same notebook she'd been doodling in yesterday.

"Hey, Catherine!" Nancy called out.

Catherine glanced up and slammed the notebook shut. "Oh, hey. I've gotta go, my mom's waiting for me outside—" she began.

Nancy pulled the teething ring out of her

pocket and held it out to Catherine. "This is yours, right?" she said. "I mean, it belongs to your baby brother, right?"

Catherine stared in shock at the teething ring. "His name's Cody," she said after a moment. "How . . . I mean, where did you get that?"

Bess frowned at Catherine. "You dropped it in Violet's cubby when you stole her Make-a-Pet bunny!"

Catherine's eyes grew enormous. "I . . . didn't steal it," she said in a voice barely above a whisper. "I was just *looking* at it. I didn't mean to take it."

Yes! Nancy thought. They had found their thief. "So what happened?" she asked Catherine.

Catherine sighed. "I was saving my allowance so I could buy a Make-a-Pet bunny," she explained. "I finally had enough. But then last week I accidentally broke one of Cody's stupid toy trucks. My parents made me spend my bunny money to replace it. So now I can't buy a Make-a-Pet!"

"So you just decided to steal somebody else's?" George said incredulously.

"No! I mean—that is—I saw Hoppity at Deirdre's house on Sunday, and on Monday during show-and-tell," Catherine explained.

"She was so cute! So after lunch . . . I was walking down the hall with my bathroom pass. I noticed Hoppity just sitting there in Violet's cubby. I stopped and picked her up, just for a second, just so I could see her up close." She added, "I remember Cody's stupid teething ring was in my pocket that day. He likes to hide stuff in weird places. It must have fallen out."

Nancy thought about Scott's toy dinosaur, which he had hidden in George's coat pocket.

"Then the bell rang, and all of a sudden everyone was in the hallway," Catherine continued. "Violet, too. I know I should have put Hoppity back. But I just kind of panicked and put Hoppity in my backpack. I was afraid Violet would see me with Hoppity and get supermad at me."

"Why didn't you just put Hoppity back in Violet's cubby, like, the next day or something?" George pointed out.

"I was going to!" Catherine insisted. "But

later that night I realized Hoppity wasn't in my backpack anymore. I think Cody might have found her and hidden her someplace. I asked him about it, but he doesn't know how to talk yet, so he couldn't tell me. I looked all over the house too. But I couldn't find Hoppity anywhere!" She looked as though she were about to burst into tears.

Nancy thought for a moment. "Hey, Catherine? Do you have still have those bunny drawings in your notebook?"

Catherine nodded. "Uh-huh. Why?"

"I think I know how we can find Hoppity," Nancy replied.

In the Spanglers' toy-filled living room, Catherine's baby brother blinked at Nancy, Bess, George, and Catherine.

"Hi, Cody. Can you help us find the bunny?" Nancy asked him in a friendly voice.

Cody blinked again.

"Catherine, what is this about?" Mrs. Spangler

called out. She was in the dining room, setting the table for dinner.

"Cody's helping us with something. I'll explain later," Catherine replied.

Nancy took Catherine's notebook from her and flipped to one of the pages filled with bunny drawings. "Bunny," Nancy repeated, showing the drawings to Cody. "Where is the bunny?"

"Boppy!" Cody squealed excitedly.

Catherine nodded eagerly. "That's right. Boppy! Where did you put Catherine's boppy?" She pointed to herself.

"Boppy!" Cody squealed again. Then he began toddling in the direction of the hallway.

"I've got him, Mom," Catherine said as she, Nancy, Bess, and George followed Cody.

"I wonder where he's going?" George whispered.

"I don't know. But wherever it is, I hope Hoppity is there," Bess whispered back.

After a few minutes Cody paused in front of

a tall terra-cotta umbrella stand. He put his chubby fingers on the rim of the stand and peered inside.

Nancy peered inside too. She saw several rolled-up black umbrellas, a doll, a graham cracker, a baby rattle . . . and a scrunched-up Make-a-Pet bunny with peanut butter on one ear. It was Hoppity!

"Here she is!" Nancy announced gleefully. She plucked Hoppity out of the umbrella stand and held her up.

"Boppy!" Cody shouted.

"That's right—boppy!" Nancy said happily. "Thank you for helping us find her, Cody."

"Hoppity, you're going home!" Bess told the bunny.

A few nights later Nancy snuggled under the blankets in her bed and opened up her purple detective notebook. Mocha Chip was tucked in beside her, and Chocolate Chip was curled up on the floor, snoring softly.

Nancy wrote:

Well, the Clue Crew has wrapped up another case. The Case of the Missing Bunny!

Violet was so happy to have Hoppity back. Catherine told her how sorry she was and explained everything.

Plus, the Petopia contest is over. Gaby won. That wasn't a big surprise. But it was a surprise when she said that she was going to use the prize money to take everyone out for ice cream at Double Dip. Yum! And she offered us all free Petopia lessons too. We had our first lesson this morning. I think I finally figured out a way to make Natasha defeat that mean old fire-breathing dragon.

Mystery solved!

Nancy made a special bed for Mocha Chip to sleep in. You can make a cozy little bed for your favorite stuffed animal too!

You will need:

A shoe box big enough for your stuffed animal. You might need an extra-big shoe box made for adult-size boots. (You could also use a cardboard box with the flaps cut off.)

Paper and/or other materials to cover the box. Think pretty tissue paper, tinfoil, fabric scraps, construction paper, brown grocery bags, old newspapers, magazine clippings, and computer printouts. Use your imagination!

Glue or a glue stick

Alphabet stickers or small, sparkly star or dot stickers

Scissors (Have an adult help you use these!)

A ruler or tape measure

An old, soft blanket that your parents will let you cut up (You could also use old scarves or other clothing, or old towels.)

Let's get started!

❀ First cover the outside (and inside) of your box with tissue paper, tinfoil, magazine clippings, etc., using glue or a glue stick to secure the materials. The end result should look like a funky collage.

❀ Once all the surfaces are dry, put your stuffed animal's name on the outside of the box using alphabet stickers. (You could also spell out its name with small, sparkly star or dot stickers.)

❀ With the scissors (and with an adult's help!), cut up an old, soft blanket into two pieces. One piece should completely line the inside of your box. (A ruler or tape measure might help.) The other piece can be smaller, serving as a blankie for tucking in your stuffed animal at night. (Feel free to use old scarves, towels, or other comfy cloths.)

Nighty night!

A Fun Fact

Bess says that Itty Bitty is always taking a cat-nap. But did you know that real kitties sleep about thirteen to eighteen hours a day? *Yawwwn!*

NANCY DREW AND THE CLUE CREW

Test your detective skills with more Clue Crew cases!

FROM ALADDIN • PUBLISHED BY SIMON & SCHUSTER

SECRET FILES
THE HARDY BOYS®

Follow the trail with Frank and Joe Hardy
in this new chapter book mystery series!

BY FRANKLIN W. DIXON

FROM ALADDIN • PUBLISHED BY
SIMON & SCHUSTER